D0835296

The Pope's
CAT

The story of a stray that was born
on the Via della Conciliazione
in Rome, is adopted by the Pope, and how she then runs the
Vatican from museum to floorboard. For ages six and up.

A NEW SERIES

This volume to be followed by
Margaret's Night in St. Peter's
(A Christmas Story)

The Pope's
CAT

JON M. SWEENEY
Illustrated by ROY DELEON

PARACLETE PRESS
BREWSTER, MASSACHUSETTS

2018 First Printing
The Pope's Cat
Text copyright © 2018 by Jon M. Sweeney
Illustrations copyright © 2018 by Roy DeLeon
ISBN 978-1-61261-935-4

This is a work of fiction. The author has used the real titles of Pope and
Holy Father in the sense in which they are normally understood: for the
leader of the Roman Catholic Church who resides in Vatican City; but
no historical Pope or Holy Father, past or present, is intended. That said,
the Queen of England and her husband, Prince Philip, make a cameo
appearance.

The Paraclete Press name and logo (dove on cross) are trademarks of
Paraclete Press, Inc.

LIBRARY OF CONGRESS CATALOGING-IN-PUBLICATION DATA
Names: Sweeney, Jon M., 1967- author. | DeLeon, Roy, illustrator.
Title: The Pope's cat / Jon M. Sweeney ; illustrated by Roy DeLeon.
Description: Brewster, Massachusetts : Paraclete Press, [2018] | Series: The
    pope's cat ; 1 | Summary:"The story of a stray cat that was born on the
    Via della Conciliazione in Rome. She is adopted by the Pope, and
she then runs the Vatican from museum to floorboard."-- Provided by
publisher.
Identifiers: LCCN 2017050204 | ISBN 9781612619354 (trade paper)
Subjects: | CYAC: Cats--Fiction. | Popes--Fiction. | Catholics--Fiction. |
    Christian life--Fiction. | Rome (Italy)--Fiction. | Vatican City--Fiction.
Classification: LCC PZ7.1.S9269 Po 2018 | DDC [E]--dc23
LC record available at https://lccn.loc.gov/2017050204

10 9 8 7 6 5 4 3 2 1
All rights reserved. No portion of this book may be reproduced, stored
in an electronic retrieval system, or transmitted in any form or by any
means—electronic, mechanical, photocopy, recording, or any other—
except for brief quotations in printed reviews, without the prior permission
of the publisher.

Published by Paraclete Press
Brewster, Massachusetts
www.paracletepress.com
Printed in the United States of America

To Margaret, Mary, and Anne.
—Jon

To the Artist Within us all.
—Roy

CHAPTER 1

People walk by Maria's Roma Gelato stand every day without noticing the cat sitting on the cobblestones. Actually, she isn't so much sitting as she is lounging in the shade provided by Maria's trash cans. But the people are too busy. They are talking, rushing across the Via della Conciliazione, often with lunch in hand, and obviously thinking about other things—other than . . .

What is this little cat doing in the midst of busy Rome?

Who is she?

Where does she live?

She lives right here, on the streets, usually near the Roma Gelato, but sometimes under the back porch of Anthony's fish market around the corner. That's where Anthony's cooks throw out the scraps every night into a large, blue dumpster. Yum!

The busy people on the Via della Conciliazione also have no idea that this stray Roman cat is about to become the most famous cat in the whole world.

She used to be just another feline on the streets.

A "menace to good society," as the mayor of Rome said once in a speech, announcing a campaign to rid the great city of every stray animal. He sent dog-catchers and cat-catchers in tiny vans to every neighborhood each evening after dark for two weeks straight, rounding up strays by the hundreds.

But that was before this Pope was elected.

Our cat was there in St. Peter's Square, among the thousands of people who stood waiting for the announcement from the Sistine Chapel of the election of a new pope—the man who would lead the worldwide Roman Catholic Church. No one saw her that day, either. It was as if she was invisible. But she was there at people's feet making sure not to get stepped on, and she appreciated all the spare food they eventually left behind. She feasted that night!

It was three weeks after the election of the new Pope that they first met.

He was walking outside the Vatican early one morning.

You see, the Pope loves
  to escape
    the thick walls
      of the Vatican
        from time to time,
         and he often
         sneaks out a
         back door to catch
         the morning
         sunrise.

The Pope likes to hear the birds singing and see the city before it wakes up. Also, there are no tourists, there, at dawn.

Later in the day, he couldn't possibly just stroll along the Via della Conciliazione. He never gets to buy a gelato from a stand like Maria's. People would shout his name, run to catch up with him, or touch his clothes, or ask him for a special blessing.

They would surround him until he couldn't move an inch further.

That's why he likes these mornings. So quiet.

On this particular day, as the sun was just coming up over the roofs of the buildings, there was the little stray cat crouched behind the trash cans, tilting her face to catch some of the warm rays. She also enjoys those early morning quiet moments.

"Here, kitty," the Pope gently said, when he saw her. He noticed that she had no collar. But she turned away, nose in the air.

"I see that you also enjoy a beautiful sunrise," he added. Then he said, "Oh come come, little kitty."

But she lifted her tail, as cats will do, as if to say, *Thank you, but no.*

How refreshing! thought the Pope, who after a few weeks in his new job was already weary of all the secretaries and assistants who said "Yes" to him all day long, and who waited on his every word. How he longed to spend time with the good friends he had before he had to put on the papal robe! Or, simply, visit a gelato stand.

So, he smiled at the cat's reluctance. Then, he got down on his hands and knees, right there on the sidewalk. No one was around. No one was there but the two of them.

"Vieni qui, dolcezza," the Pope said, just above a whisper, in Italian. (That means, "Come here, sweetness.")

That got her attention.

She turned back toward him, saw his open face and his hands outstretched. Slowly, she walked toward him. Then she stopped just short of where he was crouching on the sidewalk.

"Dai!", he said gently (which sounds like dah-yee; it is an Italian expression that means "Come on!" or "Please?!").

She couldn't resist the warm look on his face. So, she took the last step toward him and rubbed up against his forearm. The Pope picked her up in his arms. Then he said, "What's your name, sister?"

She purrrrrrrrrred.

A minute later and this little stray cat was tucked inside the cassock of this Pope, and he was walking with her back inside the Vatican apartments. The only person who saw what happened was a single Swiss Guard outside the back door, and he pretended not to notice.

Once inside, the Pope set our cat down on a couch in his apartment.

"You look hungry," he said, and reached in a cupboard for a box of sugar cookies that he keeps there.

"These are delicious," he said, as he took out three and placed them on a plate on the table in front of her.

"Eat," he suggested. "You'll like these. I do."

At first, she only licked them. *Mmmm*, they were good.

Within a few seconds, though, she was gobbling them up in just a few bites. Then she settled back on the couch, looking quite satisfied, licking her whiskers of all the extra sugar.

A minute after that and she was turning around and around, plunging her feet into the cushions, preparing to settle herself in a ball in a comfortable corner. She already felt at home.

The Pope, then, had to leave for breakfast in another room. While he was there, he happened to mention to the others at breakfast that he had made a friend that morning.

"Who is it?" they asked him.

"A beautiful girl," the Pope said, and they all smiled, imagining that a distinguished family had come for an audience with the Pope already that day. They wondered who the girl in the distinguished family might be. Meanwhile, at breakfast the Pope kept wondering how his new friend was doing back in his apartment. By the time he returned there thirty minutes later, she was sound asleep on the couch.

He looked at her lovingly.

"Margaret," he said quietly to himself.

"I shall call you 'Margaret.'"

CHAPTER 2

Popes are busy every day with appointments, formal visits, interviews with the press, and serious matters having to do with international politics. A pope, after all, is a head of state, sort of like a president or a prime minister. But since popes are also religious leaders, they are busy with daily Masses, hearing confessions, and reading and writing.

On the day that the Pope first met Margaret, he was to have lunch in the formal dining room with the Queen of England. She was bringing along her husband, Prince Philip, the Duke of Edinburgh, plus twenty some other people. Many of the Curia were going to be there, too—those are the hundreds of Vatican officials who assist popes in their work.

The Pope had never met the Queen. He was nervous. Maybe that is another reason why he took a solitary walk first thing that morning. What does someone say, after all, to a queen?

Now, he had another reason to be nervous. Little Margaret posed a bit of a problem. The Pope had to figure out what to do with her while he was away for lunch. He wasn't ready yet to tell everyone in the Vatican about his new friend. He wasn't sure if they would like the idea of a cat from the streets making a new home in the apartments of the Pope. So, he was thinking about how best to introduce her.

Soon after breakfast, the Pope left Margaret asleep in his private bedroom as he went off to St. Peter's Basilica to say Mass. There were thousands of people there at Mass. He wished he could hug them all. He loves to hug people! But he said Mass, preached a short homily, greeted as many of the people as he could, and then, suddenly, he remembered Margaret back in his apartment.

The Pope returned to his bedroom just after 12:30 in the afternoon. Margaret was still asleep on the couch.

Cats love to sleep, and Margaret was rather tired. But the Queen was coming for lunch at one o'clock. The Pope had to hurry and change his clothes.

Then there was a knock on the door.

"Holy Father, are you ready to go?" came a man's voice. The Pope knew that voice. It was his vicar Michael, who was also his good friend. Quickly, the Pope picked up Margaret and held her in his arms.

Then he said, "Come in, Father," and Michael stepped into the room. There, Michael saw the Pope sitting on his bed stroking Margaret's back. *Prrrrrrrrrrr* could be heard all over the room. It sounded as if someone had left a machine running.

The Pope smiled at Michael.

"She's purring," he said.

"I hear that," Michael said.

"But who is this?" he added.

"Margaret. She is called 'Margaret.'
I brought her in this morning."

"Hmmm. Did you?" Michael said.

I'm not sure he believed his eyes.

"Yes. Isn't she beautiful?" the Pope replied.

"She is. Where, again, did she come from?" Michael asked.

"The street," said the Pope.

"What will we do with her?"

"I think she will live here," the Pope said.

"She will?"

"Yes." And with that, the Pope set her back down gently on a pillow at the head of the bed. Then he rose to leave, and together with Michael walked out of the apartment to go and meet the Queen.

Margaret remained in a cozy ball for another minute or so. Then she picked up her head and looked around. Lush furniture and beautiful drapery filled the room.

She had never been in a room like this before. She had, in fact, never once sat quietly in a room of any kind. A cat from the streets, Margaret was used to running for her life most of the time, escaping from dogs in alleyways, as well as bad children who seem to think it is funny to throw rocks and other things at her, just because she's a stray.

Suddenly, she thought, *Wait a minute. Am I no longer a stray?*

Here she sat in the Pope's beautiful apartment in the middle of the Vatican, which is surrounded by a high brick wall that no cat could ever hope to climb over.

She looked around some more and noticed sunshine pouring in through the windows. She jumped off the bed and leaped onto a table in front of the large center window overlooking the plaza below. The lamp on the table wobbled just a bit when she jumped up, but then it settled back into its place. Margaret didn't notice this. She was pressing her pink nose against the glass.

She looked down, way down, into the plaza, and saw all the people looking back up toward her.

Can they see me? she wondered. She took a step back and flipped off the table. A second later, she jumped back up, and looked again.

It was at that moment that Margaret noticed something important. Michael and the Pope had left the door slightly ajar.

CHAPTER 3

Margaret crept stealthily toward the door and peeked around the corner into the hall. She saw a young man standing there at attention, like a soldier. He was wearing funny, striped, baggy pants, a blouse with floppy sleeves, and a beret on his head. It was another one of those Swiss Guards who watch for the safety of the Pope day and night. He looked very serious. The Swiss Guards are always looking straight ahead, as if they are staring at the wall in front of them.

Cats, in contrast, are low to the ground, and cats can move quietly. Did you know that a cat can walk right past you and you might not even hear it? It is true. Margaret left the bedroom.

Slowly . . . and quietly . . . she walked down the hall, making not a sound.

The Swiss Guard man did not even twitch.

Down the stairs she scampered, quickly now, because she began to smell the delicious aromas of butter and fish and fresh bread coming from the kitchen. Wonderful things were cooking for this party of royal guests, and the direction of the food must be where the Pope had gone to meet the Queen.

After walking down another hall, and then another, Margaret finally found a large rectangular ballroom where there were more than a hundred people standing and talking. Margaret was near the front of the room. She couldn't see the Pope among all the people, but she saw the tables where everyone was going to sit and she chose the closest one to where she was standing.

She bolted towards it. Without anyone in the room noticing, she ran and slid under its long skirt. There, she waited.

A few minutes went by. It was difficult to wait. Most of all, Margaret wanted to find the food!

Glasses were clinking. People were talking and laughing. At one point, she heard the Pope's voice near to where she was hiding. Then she saw his shoes from under the table. A few moments later, a bell gently rang.

Everyone began to sit down, and after another minute there were feet all around Margaret. Quickly, she clung to the pedestal of the table, hanging on to it with her claws so that she wouldn't get stepped on. Then, with everyone settled, she looked around and realized that she was seated in front of a chair holding someone who was wearing a long blue dress. The dress smelled pretty.

Now, Margaret wasn't used to being around pretty smelling things. She was used to stinky things, and she liked them.

Sometimes Anthony at the fish market would give her what was left of a large tuna, after the steaks were cut off it by his cooks, or a little dish of sardines. She would slop them up quickly. *Ummm,* her mouth began to water as she thought of these things.

But, pretty things—they usually made her sneeze.

Margaret poked her head out from under the large blue dress in order to take a deep breath of fresh air. She remembered what the Pope had said to Michael about wanting to wait for the right time to introduce her to the people in the Vatican. She didn't want to reveal herself.

Then, she poked her head out from under the table just a little bit further.

She looked up and saw the Pope looking down at her with kindly eyes. He was sitting right beside the woman in the blue dress! The Pope was the only one who seemed to notice how she had run into the room. As he was bending down and looking at her, about to say something, Margaret suddenly knew that she couldn't help it: she was about to sneeze.

I'll run out of the room, she thought. *There, I'll sneeze.*

So, she bolted from under the table, toward the door. But the second she started to run, a man was standing up in front of her, with a microphone about to speak. He was in her way, and when he saw her, he said, "Oh my!" and reached out his hands to try and catch her.

Margaret wasn't about to let anyone catch her!

So, she ran in the other direction, jumped up on the dais, and...then...she...couldn't...help...it... It was coming.... *Kechew! Kechew! Kechew!*

Her entire body shook each time she sneezed, and her eyes closed tightly. After the third sneeze, she had her own spit on her nose and forehead. She was embarrassed and used her paw to wipe it off. Then, her other paw.

Then, Margaret looked out at the crowd to see what was happening. There she was, on the stage at the front of the ballroom set for the Pope's luncheon with the Queen, with about two hundred pairs of eyes looking right back at her.

Margaret heard a few people gasp. One woman screamed. The man with the microphone was slowly walking toward her.

At that moment, the Pope stood up, laughing, and smiling. He walked over to the stage where Margaret was still cleaning herself, and he picked her up. He held her up to his face and then turned towards everyone.

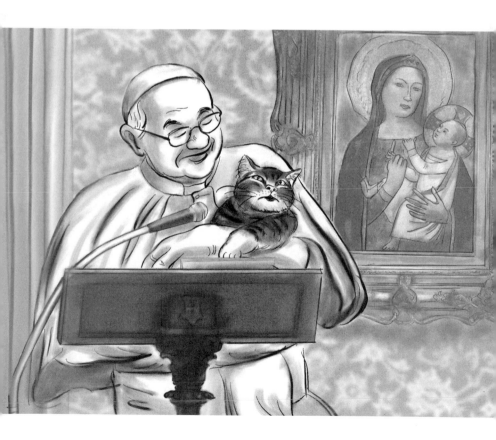

"Your Majesty, Prince Philip, my friends, I'd like to introduce you all to Margaret," he said. Everybody was watching, and then everyone began to applaud. The Pope took Margaret with him back to his table and they sat down.

The Queen smiled broadly and leaned over to say hello to Margaret. The Queen had been the one wearing the blue dress!

"How precious," the Queen said, reaching her hand towards Margaret. She had many beloved animals in her own home.

"*Kechew!*" Margaret responded. And then, quickly, "*Kechew! Kechew!*"

"Oh, I see," said the Queen. "She seems to not like the perfume I am wearing." And then, leaning over to the Pope, she added, "I don't much like it, either."

And so, the Pope arranged for Margaret to have her own large bowl of *spaghetti alle vongole*—that's spaghetti with clams!—at her very own table just inside the kitchen.

CHAPTER 4

From that day forward, Margaret and the Pope have been close friends, and she will often accompany him to meetings and to meals.

At breakfast, Margaret enjoys oatmeal with lots of whole milk and fresh berries. Before lunch, the Pope will often pull out that box of sugar cookies and give her one. And lunch and dinner usually include some kind of fish or clams or sauce that the people in the kitchen know that Margaret would most enjoy.

Not everyone in the Vatican, however, is happy about her presence there. Some people say, "She doesn't belong here," and "We are doing serious work. We don't have time for a kitty." Others say, "She is a creature of the streets. Isn't she dirty?" The Pope doesn't hear people say these things. They usually say them when he and Margaret are not around.

There was one occasion, however, only a few days after the incident with the Queen, when the Pope heard someone suggest that Margaret should probably have a check-up. He thought that was a fine idea, and a member of the Curia who is also the Pope's personal physician, was asked by the Pope to come examine Margaret, to make sure that she was healthy.

"It is for your good, sweetie," the Pope told her, and although Margaret doesn't like people poking at her, she allowed the nice man from the Curia to examine her closely.

He looked inside her mouth, at her teeth, and into her eyes. He spread the claws on her feet, looking carefully for any cuts or infections, and he looked closely at her skin, spreading her fur in several places in order to see the skin clearly. All the while, the doctor wrote notes with a pen on a medical chart.

"Bene, bene," he said to the Pope a couple of times. *Bene* means good.

Then the doctor looked inside both of Margaret's ears. He wrote something down quickly on the chart. Then, he said, "She is in good health, Holy Father. But she has mites."

"Mites?" the Pope cried. "What are mites?"

"Bugs. In her ears," the man said. "She needs a bath."

So, together, the physician from the Curia and the Pope filled a tub with warm water and a little soap that would be gentle on Margaret's skin and fur. They scrubbed her, just a bit, and even though cats don't usually like to get wet, Margaret seemed to enjoy the bath all the same. She had never been so clean!

That was weeks ago. Since then, Margaret and the Pope have spent time together every day and the members of the Curia, and the Swiss Guards, have been getting used to Margaret's presence throughout the Vatican.

Most of all, Margaret and the Pope enjoy the mornings.

The Pope likes to wake up early, just as he did on the day that he and Margaret first met.

Just the other day, he wanted to go for a walk outside on the street. Margaret was just then waking up, too. So the Pope picked her up in his arms and held her close to his chest, stroking her back the way that she liked.

As they left the apartment, they passed two Swiss Guards, both of whom pretended not to notice, and a few minutes later, together, Margaret and the Pope saw the sunrise over the pink and white buildings on the Via della Conciliazione.

THE END

ABOUT THE AUTHOR

Jon M. Sweeney is an author, husband, and father of four. "One of my favorite contemporary spiritual writers," according to James Martin, SJ, Sweeney has been interviewed on many television programs including CBS Saturday Morning, Fox News, and PBS's Religion and Ethics Newsweekly. His popular history *The Pope Who Quit: A True Medieval Tale of Mystery, Death, and Salvation*, was optioned by HBO and may soon be developed into a film. He's the author of thirty other books, as well, including *The Complete Francis of Assisi, When Saint Francis Saved the Church*, the winner of an award in history from the Catholic Press Association, and *The Enthusiast: How the Best Friend of Francis of Assisi Almost Destroyed What He Started*. This is his first book for children. He speaks often at literary and religious conferences, and churches, writes regularly for *America* in the US and *The Tablet* in the UK, and is active on social media (Twitter @ jonmsweeney; Facebook jonmsweeney).

ABOUT THE ILLUSTRATOR

Roy DeLeon is an Oblate of St. Benedict, spiritual director, yoga instructor, graphic designer, and professional visual artist. He is also the author of *Praying with the Body*. This is his first book for children. Roy lives in Bothell, Washington, with his wife, Annie.

COMING OCTOBER 1, 2018

The *Pope's* **CAT** series . . .   **BOOK TWO**

Margaret's
Night in St. Peter's
(A Christmas Story)

Bang! Slam! Boom! Loud sounds in St. Peter's Square had been going on for nearly an hour already. Margaret was annoyed, because as you may know, cats like to sleep. A lot.

The apartment where Margaret lives with the Pope, ever since he adopted her off the streets of Rome, looks out onto St. Peter's Square. And the noises down there kept waking Margaret up.

She rolled over, covering her ears with her paws.

A few minutes later, the sounds began again, as more trucks arrived to unload even more chairs. *Beep, beep, beep, beep* went the trucks as they backed up to where men in yellow jackets were waiting to unload them. Then came *Bang! Slam! Boom!* all over again, as the men arranged the chairs in rows facing the portico of St. Peter's Basilica.

All of this was in preparation for a special event to take place the following day, Christmas.

978-1-61261-936-1 | Illustrated in full-color | $9.99

Available through your local bookseller
www.paracletepress.com; 1-800-451-5006